MY WEIRD STORIES

MY WEIRD STORIES

Copyright 2024@ Fariel Ahsan.

Designed by: Fariel Ahsan

Paperback ISBN 979-8-3345-8522-5

SECOND EDITION

Price U.S.A. $9.99

Second Edition

Second Edition Note

This updated version includes two new stories, "The Hiking Mishap" and "The Flying Object", which were inadvertently left out of the first edition. Additional changes include text and book formatting.

Acknowledgement

Dear, Nora (Bubu), Fima Bhabi, Jeremy and Grandpa Paul:

Thank you so much for helping me with this book. Your contributions add a unique perspective to the book, thank you. Your artistic abilities are awe-inspiring, and I would never be able to draw something even remotely close to as good as yours. Without your illustrations, my book would be bland and incomplete. I love the drawings so much and I will never forget it (you probably won't let me forget it). Thanks to Grandpa for reviewing the manuscript and giving a thumbs-up!

Again, thank you for your efforts to enhance and help me assemble my book. You are the best!

-Sincerely, Fariel

For Mom:

My mom always thought I was a good writer, and I didn't. I always thought my writing was average, and that I only had to do it for school. Then she gave me the idea to write a book. At first, I said "No. My writing is not that good, it would take too long, and I don't want to," then she bribed me, and well, that worked, well. Even though I was bribed to write this book, I've had so much fun writing it and drawing pictures with my friends that I want to say genuinely, thank you. I never would have thought of this without you, and that's just it. Here you go, ma.

STORIES BY FARIEL AHSAN

Contents

The Secret Jungle

Deep in the mountains of Peru, there was a lush jungle. The jungle wasn't ordinary, as it was known for being mysterious and magical. The Kualo jungle was filled with traps, out to capture every being who attempted to cross the borderline. The jungle wished for all animals within to be kept safe from humans, and every tale about someone who entered the jungle never ended well. In the heart of the Kualo jungle, hidden beneath the thick canopy of leaves, there stood an ancient temple, overgrown with vines and leaves. This temple was home to a powerful artifact known as the "Scepter of Wisdom." The Scepter was rumored to possess the ability to communicate with the soul of the jungle, granting its knowledge and control over the natural world. Maria is a fearless explorer with a deep respect for the natural world. She had spent years studying the Kualo jungle, its plants and animals, and its deep history.

Unlike many who trekked into the jungle seeking fortune or glory, Maria had a different purpose. She believed that the Scepter of Wisdom could be the key to understanding and preserving the delicate balance of the jungle's ecosystem. Maria was driven by a desire to fill the gap between humans and nature, to protect the jungle from those who wanted to exploit its natural resources. With her backpack filled with notebooks, and scientific instruments, she began her expedition to uncover the secrets of the Kualo jungle. As Maria crept deeper into the jungle's lush vegetation, she encountered its various risks, from quicksand to venomous creatures and complex traps, but Maria's knowledge and respect for the jungle allowed her to navigate these dangers with caution and perseverance. During her journey, she formed a bond with an injured baby jaguar she rescued from a trap. She named the young jaguar "Soul," and together, they became companions.

Soul's keen instincts and Maria's scientific expertise fit each other perfectly, forging a partnership that would be extremely helpful in the journey to find the Scepter. After trekking for 3 hours, they took a break to have a snack and some water.

While devouring a pack of crackers, Soul heard a small crunching sound. Believing that they were just the crackers he was eating, he ignored the sound, until it happened again. He signaled to Maria that something might be approaching them.

Believing it could be a predator, Maria slowly backed away, until the thing making the sound could be visible. It wasn't a predator, but it was a boy from a nearby native tribe.

The boy spoke a language Maria had heard of, but couldn't understand, then she remembered that she had brought a book that explained sentences, words, and phrases from languages native to the Kualo jungle. She quickly grabbed the book from her backpack and began to decipher the boy's sentences. The boy said, "If you are looking for the Scepter, I can tell you the path, but only if you can answer my questions correctly." Maria stared at the young boy with curiosity and nodded, accepting his challenge. She had spent her life studying the Kualo jungle and its mysteries. She believed she was well-prepared to answer the boy's questions.

The boy, who said his name was Tariq, began his series of questions. "First question," he said in his native language, which Maria now partly understood with the help of her book, "What is the guardian spirit of the Kualo jungle, and how is it said to protect this place?" Maria thought carefully before responding, "The guardian spirit of the Kualo jungle is known as Ezula," also known as a majestic jaguar. It is said that Ezula watches over the jungle, guiding lost animals to safety and making sure that those who enter with harmful intentions face its power through the jungle's natural traps and obstacles." Tariq nodded. "Well done. Second question: What is the most sacred tree in the Kualo jungle, and what does it hold in our culture?" Maria knew the answer to this question as well. "The most sacred tree in the Kualo jungle is the Heart Tree. It is said to be between the earth and the spirit world. The culture believes that the spirits of their family live in its branches, and it is a symbol of the connections of all living things." Tariq smiled and continued, "Impressive. Now, for the last question:"

What is the true purpose of the Scepter of Wisdom, and why do you seek it?" Maria took a deep breath, realizing the importance of this question. "The Scepter of Wisdom is believed to hold the power to communicate with the soul of the jungle, gaining its knowledge and wisdom.

I seek it not for personal gain, but to use its power to protect the Kualo jungle from those who would harm it. I believe that we have to ensure that this ecosystem is safe for the future." Tariq smiled and said, "You have answered all my questions correctly, Maria. You are a friend to the jungle, and I will help you find the path to the Scepter of Wisdom. But remember, it is not a power to be taken lightly. Use it wisely and with respect for the jungle's delicate ecosystem." Maria thanked Tariq for his help. With Soul and Tariq by her side, she continued her journey deeper into the Kualo jungle, now with not only her scientific knowledge, and Soul's quick instincts but also the help of a guide who understood the jungle's secrets.

Together, they got closer to the ancient temple and the Scepter of Wisdom, with the hope of creating a connection between humanity and the heart of the jungle that had remained hidden for centuries.

The Secret Jungle

A Road trip of terror

L eland had always wanted to go on a road trip. Since she was three, she had heard of her grandparents' awesome adventures, which she wanted to experience as well. When she turned 12 years old, her parents surprised her with the news that they were going on a road trip together as a family. She could barely contain her excitement as they sat around the kitchen table, unfolding the large map of the United States.

Her father, John, was an engineer who had meticulously planned their route. Her mother, Emily, was a history nerd, eager to explore the cultural landmarks along the way. Leland, with her curiosity, couldn't wait to see the world beyond her small town.

They packed their car with suitcases, snacks, and a sense of adventure. The first day of their road trip was filled with laughter, music, and games as they drove through picturesque landscapes. Leland stared at the changing scenery, from rolling hills to long deserts. They stopped at roadside diners and explored roadside attractions, making memories that would last a lifetime.

But as they ventured deeper into their journey, a series of unexpected events began to unfold. It started with a sudden downpour that turned a dusty trail into a mud pit, trapping their car in the middle of nowhere. They waited for hours, hoping for another traveler to pass by, but it seemed they were alone in the remote wilderness.

Night fell, and the family huddled together inside the car, their faces filled with worry. The rain continued to pour relentlessly, making their situation even more dicey. Leland tried to stay brave, reminding herself of the stories her grandparents had told her about their own adventures, but fear gnawed at her.

Hours turned into a long, sleepless night. When dawn finally broke, the rain had stopped, and the family decided to leave the car behind and set out on foot to find help. They trekked through the soggy wilderness, their shoes caked with mud, and their spirits dampened by uncertainty.

Just as they were about to give up, they stumbled upon an old, abandoned cabin deep in the woods. It was a curious and eerie sight, overgrown with ivy and seemingly untouched for years. Desperate for shelter, they cautiously entered the cabin, unsure of what they might find inside.

Inside the cabin, the air was thick with the scent of damp wood. Cobwebs covered the corners of the room. Leland's heart raced as she looked around, feeling a strange mix of curiosity and fear. Emily, ever the history enthusiast, couldn't resist examining the cabin clearly. She discovered an old journal on an old wooden table.

The handwriting was faded, but she managed to read a few sentences. The journal belonged to a previous owner of the house who had documented their own experiences in this remote location. As Emily read aloud, a ghastly figure emerged from the page of the book. It was a mysterious creature. The family began to slowly walk backward to try and leave the cabin. As the creature realized their attempt to escape, he muttered something that sounded like gibberish, which the family hadn't noticed. Once they got close to the door, they tried to run away, but the door was locked. They immediately realized the creature had summoned the door to lock and wouldn't let them escape. They knew they had to fight or flee. Their decision would choose their fate.

Ocean 666

Living in a California beach town, 12-year-old Andrew and his family enjoyed their coastal life. Andrew had a deep love for the water, spending every free moment swimming by the beach, often in the mornings. His parents were always concerned about his safety, fearing something perilous might occur. But Andrew paid little attention to their worries. At times, he even sneaked out in the dead of night to swim in the darkness.

One night, while Andrew was swimming far from the shore, something grabbed his foot. It was a terrifying creature that capsized him and dragged him beneath the water's surface. Struggling to breathe, Andrew fought back, delivering a powerful kick to the creature, and narrowly escaping. Filled with fear, he rushed back to his house, trying to move as silently as possible, and climbed into bed.

The following morning, Andrew awoke, half-convinced that the previous night's events had been nothing more than a dream. After grabbing a quick bite to eat, he set out for some fishing by the shore, hoping to catch lunch. As he reeled in his first catch of the day, a massive snook, he noticed a mysterious reddish blob in the ocean, proving last night's horrors were not dreams. He hurriedly abandoned his fishing gear and sprinted back home.

Concerned by his strange behavior, Andrew's mother went to his room to confront him about what was troubling him. He put together a quick lie, stammering that he had encountered a box jellyfish and narrowly avoided being stung. His mother accepted the explanation, though her skepticism lingered due to the suddenness of his claim. It became evident to his parents that something was scaring their son, even if they couldn't quite pinpoint what it was.

The following day, for the first time in years, Andrew refused to leave the house. His worried father suggested a trip to the beach, and Andrew agreed, preferring the company of his dad. While fishing, they once again spotted the ominous red blob in the ocean. This time, Andrew finally admitted to his father the truth. He confessed that he had been sneaking out to swim at night and recounted the horrifying incident with the underwater creature. He also explained why he ran from the shore when he saw the red blob while fishing. His father, alarmed by the secret, immediately gathered their fishing gear, and they raced back home.

Upon arriving, they explained everything to Andrew's mother, who insisted they inform the community about the dangerous creature lurking in the ocean. After a quick drink of water and a snack, they set out to notify their neighbors. Word spread rapidly across California, and within a week, experts arrived to examine the mysterious beast.

As specialists were examining the creature, it suddenly leaped from the water, giving everyone a clear view. By passers quickly reached for their phones to capture images of the strange, massive, red, slimy creature resembling a mix of a squid and octopus. It unleashed precise inkjets, causing panic on the streets. Andrew dialed 911, and soon the police arrived along with two fire trucks. They opened fire on the creature, but it seemed immortal, not even shedding a drop of blood.

The creature's next actions were terrifying. It seized the fire trucks, placing the firefighters on Andrew's house roof before flinging the trucks into the ocean. Fearing a similar fate for their vehicles, the police officers retreated, leaving the unarmed crowd to witness the creature's rampage as it uprooted trees.

Realizing they were in grave danger, Andrew's family hastily collected their most essential belongings and fled in their hidden garage-stored car, speeding away from the unfolding chaos.

King of the Jungle

One sunny day in the jungle, the Lion, Hare, and Cobra were sitting under a tree, enjoying some juicy mangoes. Meanwhile, the Tiger was napping nearby, but the aroma of the mangoes awakened him. When he saw the fruit, he demanded that they give it to him and commanded that they go hunt a meal for him.

The Lion spoke up, "I'm tired of constantly hunting for him and giving away our food." The Hare added, "I feel the same way. Maybe there's a better way. Lion, have you considered challenging Tiger in a voting competition? The winner could become the king of the jungle." Lion thought of this idea and found the scheme a great idea.

He gathered all the animals and explained to the Tiger, "Tiger, you and I will have a competition. All the animals in the jungle will cast their votes for either you or me. The one with the most votes will become the king." Tiger laughed arrogantly, "You think you can beat me? Ha ha ha!" Undaunted, Lion continued, "I will give everyone a small slip of paper to write down their choice. A week from today, we will open the box and count the votes." The following week seemed to drag on endlessly.

On the seventh day, when it was time to open the box, a fierce storm swept through the jungle, causing trees to topple and homes to be destroyed, including Tiger's home. No one came to his aid, and Lion decided to postpone the competition for another week.

One week later, the animals gathered again, and Cobra, the judge, announced, "I've counted the votes. There are twenty-six votes for Tiger and thirty-one votes for Lion! Lion is the winner!" Lion couldn't contain his excitement. "Thank you to everyone who voted for me. I will always remember this day!" Tiger, however, wasn't convinced. He approached the box and counted, exclaiming, "Ha! What's this?" Lion asked, puzzled, "What's wrong?" Tiger replied, "Cobra lied. I found thirty-one votes for you and thirty-one votes for me. We're tied!" Lion considered this for a moment and then declared, "In that case, we will have a tiebreaker." Lion continued, "Tiger, choose 8 animals, and I will choose 8 animals. The ones we select will vote again, and the majority will determine the winner." Once the voting was complete, Lion opened the box, counted the votes, and announced, "7 votes for Tiger and 9 votes for me!" Tiger protested, "No, you can't do this! I am the king of the jungle!" Lion replied confidently, "Well, not anymore," with a smile. His friends congratulated him and said, "You defeated Tiger. That's fantastic!"

Tiger walked away with a frown and muttered, "I'll get you back for this," but he never did. Lion proved to be a better king, hunting for his own meals, and solving problems wisely. To this day, the Lion is still known as the wise king of the jungle.

The Camping Nightmare

Once upon a time, in a small town in between hills and a beautiful; lake, lived the Johnson family. Mark, the father, Emily, a loving mother, and their two children, Jake, and Lily. The family shared a deep love for the outdoors, and their yearly camping trip was their favorite tradition.

This year, they decided to venture deep into the Mystery Woods National Park, a place they had only heard tales of. Excitement bubbled within them as they loaded their camping gear into their trusty old station wagon. The journey ahead promised remarkable memories.

As they arrived at the park, they were welcomed by a lush forest teeming with life. The sun glowed through the thick canopy of trees, and the air was filled with the sweet scent of pine. The Johnsons found the perfect spot near a babbling brook, with a clearing big enough for their tent. It was a serene, setting that seemed straight out of a fairy tale.

The first day of their camping trip was all fun. They hiked along winding trails, picnicked by the lake, and marveled at the diverse wildlife. Mark, an experienced camper, taught Jake, and Lily how to build a campfire, while Emily prepared a delicious dinner of roasted marshmallows and hotdogs.

However, as the day turned into night, an ominous feeling crept over the campsite. A sudden chill in the air made the family huddle closer to the fire. Strange rustling noises echoed in the distance, and the forest seemed to close in on them.

That night, they scurried to their tent, but sleep wasn't there. The forest was alive with eerie sounds, and the children clung to their parents for comfort. Trying to reassure them, Mark whispered that it was just the forest's way of speaking.

The following morning brought more unsettling events. They woke up to find their food supplies ravaged and scattered around the campsite. There were paw prints, large and ominous, around their tent, and soon panic set in as they realized they were not alone in the woods.

With a sense of urgency, Mark decided they should pack up and leave, but as they gathered their belongings, a deep growl arose from the shadows. Emerging from the forest was a massive, territorial bear. Fear showed over them as they realized they were trapped between the bear and the brook.

Frantically, they tried to make themselves appear larger and more threatening, waving their arms and shouting. But the bear, undaunted, continued to advance. It came close enough to attack, soon breaking their tent and materials. It began to attack Mark, injuring him in the leg. It was then that Emily remembered the bear spray in their backpack. She grabbed it and, with trembling hands, sprayed a cloud of deterrent towards the bear.

The bear roared in pain and frustration, then retreated into the forest. The Johnsons were shaken but relieved. However, their camping trip had turned into a nightmare, and they couldn't ignore the dangers that lurked in these woods.

They quickly packed up their camp and hiked back to their car, constantly looking over their shoulders. The Mystery Woods National Park, once a place of wonder, had become a place of fear. They left with a new respect for nature's power and a story they would never forget.

As they drove away from the park, the family shared a glance. They knew that despite the horrific experience, their love for the outdoors would never leave, and they would be back for more adventures, hopefully with fewer unexpected twists.

2045

The year is 2045. Jack Morsly, one of the most educated scientists in the world figured out the secret to immortality. Even though this seems like it will help the world, it comes with a significant cost. And no, I don't mean money, but it involves danger, and somehow, I got involved in it. Here's what happened.

I woke up, realizing it was a Monday. I groan "Great, a brand-new week of school." I get dressed and hastily rush downstairs to make sure I'm not late for the bus. After grabbing a cookie and some water, I bring my backpack and head out, still upset that there was school that day. PE first I thought "Nice!" The bus arrived on time, which is honestly unusual. I didn't care all that much because the bell was about to ring, and I seriously did not want to be late for PE.

We started with a few warm-ups, then began. Our new unit was starting today, and was I shocked when he said" Alrighty kids, our new unit is going to be Basketball!"

I know basketball is extremely popular, but I hate it. I have despised basketball for all my life. I just don't get the point of basketball. All you do is run around and do these strange maneuvers while just throwing a ball. It's not that hard or fun. He began calling names for teams when I heard "Ralph go on the blue side and grab a penny."

Mr. Anderson began the scrimmage by blowing the whistle while I stood there on the basketball court, feeling dreadful as the game started. I wasn't focused as I mindlessly walked around like a zombie, trying not to get into the game. Little did I know that this disappointing Monday morning would turn out to be anything but regular. As the game went on, something strange happened. The sun suddenly went dark. I looked up, confused, only to see a weird portal at the far end of the basketball court.

It looked like a hologram. The portal looked a deep blue, drawing the attention of my classmates, and Mr. Anderson. Everyone stopped, forgetting about the game, and a weird shape could be seen from the portal. It was none other than Jack Morsly, the man who had found the secret to immortality. Jack Morsly looked different than any image I'd seen of him before. His hair was wild and tangled, his clothes mucky, and there was a look on his face that confused me. Without hesitation, he pulled me over. "Come here, Ralph," he said urgently. "You have no idea what's at stake here." I was worried about how he knew my name, but walked towards him anyway, my heart pounding. Mr. Anderson and my classmates watched with a mix of fear and curiosity. Jack explained, "I've discovered immortality, but it comes with a dangerous side effect, and I need your help to fix it. You have a unique power, which has a connection to this, and you must join me on a journey to save the world." I was baffled. How could I, a middle school student with a hate for basketball, be the key to solving such a crazy crisis? But the sound of urgency left me with no choice but to agree. As I stepped through the portal, leaving behind my classmates and the basketball court I despised, I had no idea what was going to happen.

As I stepped through the portal everything looked different. The sky was red, the grass was orange, and the trees were white. Jack said that the side effect of immortality wasn't solely a side effect, but also was an ancient curse. The curse wasn't something else though. The curse was immortality itself. Jack explained "You see, immortality is just painful. It's fine until you begin to grow old, and then you are stuck with that forever. You can't do anything. Luckily, you have a power within you, which I can harness using this device." He handed over a small gadget that looked like a microchip. "I invented this," Jack said, and I responded with a "cool."

He began to explain my powers. He said "You have the rare power to pause time. But you can also reverse time" I questioned him "But, how?" He said "Oh, well the reverse works b-" "N-n-no, how did I get these powers? "From your dad. You should have noticed by now. "How does he get to work on time when he leaves

1 minute before his shift?" I began to understand, and things were coming together, well, somewhat.

Jack said "To stop time, you have a code. You have to say something, which pauses everything, except me because I have this little device here. Now, think about a common sentence your parents would say when they're in a hurry," Jack explained. I thought for a moment, recalling the countless times I'd heard my dad say, "In the blink of an eye." It was a phrase he used whenever he rushed off to work or tried to finish a task quickly. Jack nodded, a hint of satisfaction in his eyes. "Exactly.

Now, focus on that phrase and repeat it in your mind." I did as he instructed, repeating, "In the blink of an eye," over and over. Suddenly, I felt a strange feeling, like time was holding its breath. Everything around me froze—the swaying trees, the rustling grass, and even Jack. It was as if the world had turned into a living photo. Jack began to move again, through the frozen silence. "Good, Ralph. You've stopped time. Now, to reverse it, simply say the same phrase again." I nodded, still trying to wrap my head around the incredible power I own. I repeated, "In the blink of an eye," and just like that, time resumed its own thing.

The red sky, orange grass, and white trees returned to motion. Jack smiled, relieved that his explanation had worked. "You see, Ralph, your rare ability is the key to reversing the curse of immortality. With your power to pause time, we can undo the effects of the immortality serum, which I have made."

As I realized the weight of the responsibility I had to keep up with, I couldn't help but wonder about the danger that was ahead. Jack had mentioned a curse, and I had no idea what kind of challenges we would face in this surreal, altered world. Still, I knew that I couldn't turn back now. Lives depended on my new abilities, literally, and together with Jack, I was determined to find a way to break the curse of immortality and save the world. Our adventure had just begun, and I had a feeling that the days of despising basketball and dreaded Mondays were behind me.

Horrific Halloween

Once upon an October evening in the cozy town of Fern, four kids named Emily, Jake, Sarah, and Ben prepared for their favorite night of the year - Halloween. They had spent weeks brainstorming the perfect costumes, and now, with their backpacks loaded with candy bags, they were ready to begin their annual trick-or-treating adventure.

The evening sky was painted with shades of orange and purple as the squad set off into their neighborhood. Houses were decorated with pumpkins, cobwebs, and ghosts, and the autumn air was filled with the scent of fallen leaves. Their laughter echoed through the streets as they went from house to house, collecting candy and watching the creative decorations.

As the night grew darker, the children arrived at the edge of town. The houses here were much older, and their yards were overgrown with twisted vines. At the end of the street was an ominous mansion known as the Holloway House.

No one in the town knew who lived there or when it had last been inhabited. Its dark windows and eerie creaks sent shivers down their spines, but curiosity got the better of them. "This is it, guys," Emily said with a wicked grin. "The spookiest house in all of Fern. Let's knock and see if they have any candy." The others hesitated for a moment, then joined Emily on the porch. She gave the heavy wooden door three knocks. A moment later, the door slowly creaked open, revealing a dimly lit hallway beyond.

"Trick or treat!" they said in unison. No one answered. The children exchanged nervous glances before taking steps inside. The hallway was covered with ancient portraits that watched their every move, and cobwebs hung from the ceiling. As they crept deeper into the mansion, they stumbled upon a room with a massive mirror. The glass was disoriented, and the reflection of their costumes twisted and distorted. Sarah's fairy wings grew to enormous, Jake's pirate hat tilted at a bizarre angle, and Ben's werewolf fangs grew to a comical size. The children gasped, their hearts racing. "This mirror was no ordinary mirror, and they realized they had stepped into something far more mysterious than they could have imagined."

They decided to retrace their steps and leave the unsettling house, but to their horror, the hallway seemed to stretch endlessly behind them. Panicking, they raced through the dark corridors, but the mansion played tricks on their senses. Rooms changed shape, doors led to nowhere, and staircases seemed to spiral infinitely. It seemed like they were trapped in a nightmare.

Hours passed, and exhaustion began to set in. Just when it seemed all hope was lost, they stumbled upon a dusty library.

On an old table, they found a leather book. Its pages were filled with symbols and drawings that seemed to match the mansion's architecture. Emily, the book nerd, examined the text and realized that the only way to escape was to solve a riddle hidden within the mansion's design. Working together, they put together the clues and, at last, reached the heart of the house—the attic. There, they discovered an ancient spell book. Emily, having studied it for a moment, managed to break the enchantment and release their friends from the mansion's grip. The house shook as if it were waking from a deep sleep, and then, with a roar, it collapsed into itself, disappearing in a cloud of dust. The four children stood amidst the ruins of the Holloway House, panting, and covered in dust.

It was over, and they had survived their Halloween adventure. They made their way back to their neighborhood, grateful for the familiar sights and sounds of Fern. As they continued their trick-or-treating, they couldn't help but glance back at the empty lot where the mansion had stood, forever changed by their Halloween night. It was a night they would never forget, a night when their thirst for adventure had led them to the strangest, spookiest, and most memorable Halloween ever.

The Human Chase

On a pleasant October night, Julian abruptly awoke from his sleep. He had been startled by loud, banging noises from outside. With a little fear, he tiptoed downstairs to investigate. He peered out the window. What he saw sent shivers down his spine, a real ALIEN! His scream echoed as he struggled to realize the scene unfolding before him.

He knew he had to escape, quick! With much confusion, Julian hurriedly put on his shoes and fled the house. A crowd of aliens ran after him but couldn't quite catch up to him. As he ran, he found himself chased by not just one, but hundreds, maybe even thousands of these crazy creatures. In all the mayhem, Julian stumbled upon his best friend, Nolan. They saw each other, and Nolan explained the strange situation. "For centuries," he began, "aliens have lived within the Earth's core, and tonight, they've launched an attack. We need to escape—quickly." Julian started to panic; It was pure chaos. Looking behind them they saw the aliens were catching up, Julian and Nolan almost got captured, but they knew it was only a matter of time before they closed in with victory. With urgency, they made a plan: to create a stone replica and place it on the top of a mountain, so it looked like they were still there.

By the time the aliens reached the summit, Julian and Nolan would be miles away, far away from where they were. The question of how these extraterrestrials had gotten into the Earth's core remained a mystery, puzzling them as they continued their escape. As they completed making the statues, they hiked onward, ready to embark on a long journey to safety.

Their path led them through a bushy forest, where, after hours of hiking, they stumbled upon a beautiful waterfall. Nolan exclaimed, "Thank goodness! I'm parched." However, their rest was short as a mysterious figure could be seen in the distance—a fierce tiger, guarding its territory. With speed, they fled the scene, carrying water with them for the long journey ahead. Realizing they had no other option, they resolved to make their way to the United States, guiding them from a Brazilian rainforest through Central America. Meanwhile, the aliens were in the Amazon Rainforest, realizing the urgency of leaving before they gave in to the dangers lurking there. To their surprise, they stumbled upon the trail of Julian and Nolan, leading them toward Central America. Fearing the power of the U.S. military, the aliens decided to tail the two humans.

Upon reaching Mexico, Julian and Nolan encountered a kind-hearted man named Juan, who revealed a shocking truth: they were among the last surviving humans on Earth. Only those sheltered within the borders of the USA remained. Juan wanted to join them, and Julian offered to accompany him on his quest. As Julian, Nolan, and Juan progressed through Mexico, they were unaware that the aliens had reached the Mexican border. Tension came to them as they neared the U.S. border. The aliens spotted them, and the chase started. The trio rode on tigers that appeared on their path, desperately racing toward Arizona. With just meters left, they reached the safety of the U.S. border just before the government sealed it with a wall of impenetrable steel.

The aliens rushed toward the barrier and disintegrated upon contact; their weakness exposed. Julian exclaimed, "We've finally defeated the aliens! Now, we can return to Brazil." Yet, his happiness was filled with sorrow. His parents were still missing, but the reunion he wanted was about to happen. In an unexpected twist, as the U.S. government removed the metal barriers, they discovered that many people had been hiding in their homes, concealed from the aliens, and the US military had saved them, which included Julian and Nolan's parents! Tears welled up in Julian's eyes as he hugged his parents, and they celebrated their reunion with a big dinner—a reminder that even in the face of threats, humans endured. .

The Hiking Mishap

The morning sun peeked through the trees, casting welcomed light on the forest floor. Birds chirped merrily, welcoming the new day. Mark and Jake, friends since elementary school, stood at the edge of the trail, backpacks slung over their shoulders and excitement in their eyes.

"Ready for this, Jake?" Mark asked, tightening the straps of his backpack.

Born ready," Jake replied with a grin. He adjusted his baseball cap and started down the path, Mark close behind him.

The two friends had planned this hiking trip for months. Both were outdoor enthusiasts, finding thrill in nature. They'd chosen this particular trail for its beauty and the challenge it presented. The path wound through dense forests, alongside babbling brooks, and up steep inclines, promising an unforgettable adventure. They reminisced about past adventures as they walked, from camping trips in their teens to spontaneous hiking trips during college.

The forest seemed to come alive with their laughter and chatter. They were determined and focused, eager to embrace whatever the trail had in store for them. Each step felt like a renewal of their lifelong bond, strengthened by shared memories and the promise of new experiences.

As they ventured deeper into the woods, the sounds of civilization faded away, replaced by the symphony of nature. The rustling leaves, the distant call of a hawk, and the rhythmic crunch of their boots on the forest floor created a soundtrack for their journey. The air was fresh and invigorating, filling their lungs with each breath and fueling their enthusiasm.

After a couple of hours, the trail grew steeper. The friends paused at a scenic overlook, the view being breathtaking. Below them, a river winding through the forest, glistening in the sunlight.

"This is amazing," Jake said, pulling out his camera. "Let's get a picture." Mark nodded, and they posed with the stunning view behind them. After a few shots, they continued, their spirits high despite the increasing challenge. The sun rose higher in the sky, and the forest became more peaceful. The only sounds were their footsteps and the occasional crunching of leaves and sticks. They stopped for lunch at a clearing, munching on sandwiches and sipping water while enjoying the peaceful surroundings.

"Do you think we'll see any wildlife?" Mark asked, scanning the area.

"Maybe," Jake replied, packing away his lunch. "I read that there are deer, foxes, and even a few bears around here."

Mark raised an eyebrow. "Bears? Let's hope we don't run into any." They both laughed, but there was a hint of seriousness. The wilderness was beautiful, but it demanded caution.

As the afternoon wore on, the friends ventured deeper into the forest. The path narrowed, and the underbrush grew thicker. They had to navigate carefully, avoiding roots, rocks, and low-hanging branches. Suddenly, Jake stopped, his eyes wide open.

"Mark, look!" Mark followed his gaze and saw a copperhead snake slithering across the path. It was small and sleek, its scales shimmering in the light.

"Wow," Mark whispered. "I've never seen a snake like that before."

"It's beautiful," Jake agreed, pulling out his camera again. He inched closer, trying to get a good shot.

"Be careful," Mark warned. "The copperhead is a venomous snake." But before Jake could respond, the snake struck. It happened in a blur, the snake's fangs sinking into Jake's leg. He yelped in pain and stumbled back, dropping his camera. "Jake!" Mark shouted, rushing to his friend's side. The snake slithered away, disappearing into the underbrush. Jake's face was pale, and he was clutching his leg.

"It bit me," he gasped. "It really bit me."

Mark's heart pounded in his chest. He'd read about snake bites and knew they needed to act fast. He helped Jake sit down and inspected the bite. Two puncture wounds were already swelling and turning red.

"Stay calm," Mark said, trying to keep his voice steady. "We need to get you to a hospital."

He fumbled for his phone, but there was no signal. They were too deep in the forest. Mark was panicking under his breath and quickly rummaged through his backpack, pulling out the first aid kit.

"Here," he said, handing Jake a water bottle. "Drink this. We need to keep you hydrated."

Jake nodded, wincing as he took a sip. Mark wrapped a gauge tightly above the wound, hoping to slow down the spread of venom. He knew they had to get moving fast.

"Can you walk?" Mark asked, helping Jake to his feet.

Jake gritted his teeth. "I think so."

Supporting his friend, Mark began the painful journey back. Each step was a struggle, the path seeming much longer than it had earlier. Jake's condition worsened, his breathing becoming short and rapid.

"You hang in there, Jake," Mark urged. "We're going to make it."

After what felt like an eternity, they reached the scenic overlook where they'd taken pictures earlier. Mark's legs were burning, but he pushed on, driven by sheer determination.

Suddenly, they heard voices. Mark's heart leaped. "Hey!" he shouted, waving his arms. "We need help!"

A group of hikers appeared, alarmed by the sight of Jake leaning heavily on Mark. One of them, a woman with a first aid kit, rushed over.

"What happened?" she asked, examining Jake.

"A copperhead bit him," Mark explained, his voice shaky. "We need to get him to a hospital."

The woman nodded. "There's a ranger station not far from here. We have a radio and can call for help."

Relief washed over Mark. Together, they helped Jake to the ranger station. The rangers responded quickly, calling for a helicopter to airlift Jake to the nearest hospital.

As they waited, Mark sat beside his friend, holding his hand. "You're going to be okay, Jake. Just hang in there."

Jake managed a weak smile. "Thanks, Mark. I don't know what I would have done without you."

The helicopter arrived, and Jake was whisked away to safety. Mark watched it disappear into the sky, a mixture of exhaustion and relief flooding over him.

A few days later, Mark visited Jake in the hospital. His friend was recovering well, thanks to the prompt medical attention.

"Hey, hero," Jake greeted him with a grin. "Come to save me again?"

Mark laughed, relieved to see Jake's sense of humor intact. "Just checking up on you. How are you feeling?"

"Better," Jake said. "They said I was lucky. If you hadn't put that gauge around my leg, the venom could have spread throughout the entire body and stopped my heart, things could have been a lot worse."

Mark shook his head. "We were both lucky. And we're going to be more careful next time."

Jake nodded. "Definitely. But there's still going to be a next time, right?"

"Absolutely," Mark replied, smiling. "There's always another adventure waiting for us."

The bond between the two friends had been tested by the wilderness, and it had emerged stronger than ever. They knew that no matter what challenges lay ahead, they would face them together, just as they always had.

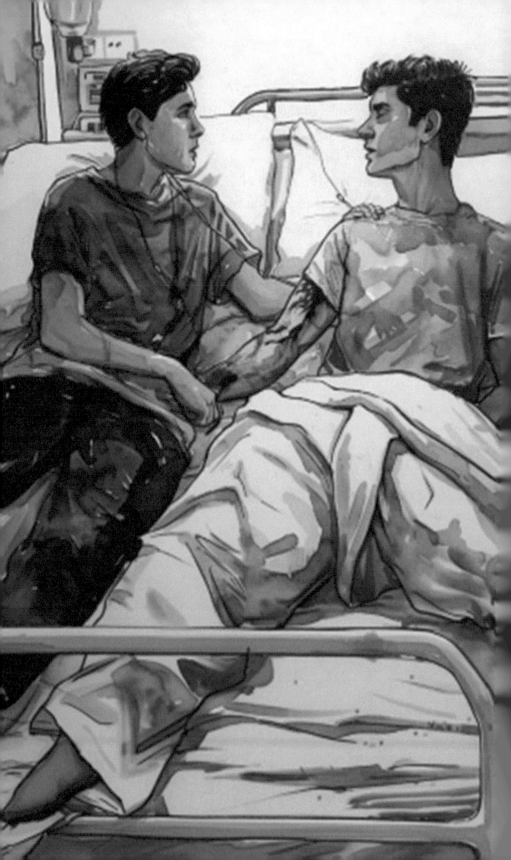

The Flying Object

Andrew woke up very early. It still seemed dark out, and he used agile movements as he tiptoed downstairs for breakfast. Although Andrew didn't like going to school as much, he was very intelligent. He turned on the fireplace and watched it begin to crackle to life. After warming up in his silent house, he sat outside on his patio as he watched the sunrise, as he waited for his old rickety bus to arrive. It was damp, but not too cold. It felt like the perfect mixture of warm and cold. The sun rose, lighting up the area and making it more clear to see.

As Andrew sat on his patio, watching the sunrise, he noticed something unusual in the sky. A distant rumble and a peculiar flickering light caught his attention. He squinted at the horizon, trying to make sense of it. Andrew's neighbor, Mr. Johnson, who was also up early for his morning jog, called out to him.

"Hey, Andrew, do you see that over there?" he asked, pointing at the sky. Andrew strained his eyes and replied,

"Yeah, it looks like some sort of strange aircraft. I've never seen anything like it before."

They continued to watch, the distant object grew closer and more menacing. The noise grew louder, and Andrew could see a massive, unidentified flying object descending rapidly toward North America. It was unlike anything the world had ever witnessed. Andrew's heart raced as he realized the potential danger this unknown craft posed to his country. Without hesitation, he sprinted back inside, dialed 911, and shouted into the phone,

"Emergency! There's an unidentified object approaching North America. We need help!" The dispatcher on the other end of the line responded,

"Stay on the line. We're sending emergency services right away." Meanwhile, Andrew's school bus arrived, but he knew he couldn't go to school that day. He hurried back outside to warn his neighbors about the impending threat. As he ran from house to house, knocking on doors and shouting, people started to emerge, and panic began to spread. Andrew's best friend, Sarah, came out of her house, and he quickly explained the situation.

"Sarah, we have to get everyone together and come up with a plan. North America is in danger, and we might be the ones who can save it!" With determination in their eyes, Andrew, Sarah, and their neighbors began to gather in the middle of the street, ready to face the unknown.

They knew that they had to work together to protect their homeland.

The object approached the area, and soon after followed 10 more of the drones.

The tension in the street grew as the group waited for the emergency services to arrive. Andrew had managed to contact the local news as well, and soon, a small crowd had gathered around the concerned residents. The object in the sky was now joined by ten more drones, and their formation was unlike anything the world had seen.

One of the neighbors, Mr. Ramirez, a retired Air Force veteran, stepped forward.

"I've seen a lot of aircraft in my time, but those things are no aircraft I've ever encountered. They could be a threat to national security." Sarah chimed in,

"We can't just stand here and wait. We need to come up with a plan. Maybe we should seek shelter or organize some kind of defense.

" Andrew nodded in agreement. "You're right, Sarah. We can't just rely on others to handle this. Let's gather information, and if it turns out to be a threat, we can take action." As the group huddled together, Mr. Johnson suggested,

"We should try to contact the local military base. They might have more information about this." Andrew called the base, and after some tense moments on the line, he explained the situation to the military personnel. They were equally baffled and concerned by the strange objects in the sky. They advised the group to stay put and cooperate with emergency services while they assessed the situation. The police and fire department had now arrived in the neighborhood.

The authorities blocked off the area, and they were in touch with higher levels of government to figure out how to handle this unprecedented threat. A local news crew arrived, and a reporter began interviewing Sarah, Andrew, and their neighbors about the situation. As the camera rolled, Sarah urged everyone watching to remain calm and stay informed.

"We don't know if these objects are a threat yet, but our community is coming together to ensure our safety." The tension was palpable as time passed, and the objects in the sky hovered ominously. Everyone continued to watch and wait, knowing that they were now a part of a situation beyond their comprehension. The military finally arrived, sending fighter jets to escort the unidentified objects away from the residential area.

With their departure, a collective sigh of relief swept through the neighborhood. As the immediate danger passed, the authorities thanked the residents for their vigilance and cooperation. The incident was shrouded in secrecy, and the official explanation was limited to a "training exercise."

Due to Andrew's actions and his taking strong responsibility, he is known to be "The Savior of Redwood.

The End

Made in the USA
Columbia, SC
18 November 2024